Picnic Time

Written by Cynthia Rider,
based on the original characters
created by Roderick Hunt and Alex Brychta
Illustrated by Alex Brychta

OXFORD
UNIVERSITY PRESS

“Picnic time!” said Dad.

Biff sat on a log.

Some sheep came.

“Run!” said Kipper.

They sat on a bridge.

Some ducks came.

"Run!" said Chip.

They sat on a wall.

Some donkeys came.

"Run!" said Biff.

They sat on a rock.

Oh no! The rain came!

Talk about the story

Tangled lines

Who will get the picnic?